THE COW BUZZED

by Andrea Zimmerman and David Clemesha

illustrated by Paul Meisel

HarperCollins*Publishers*

The Cow Buzzed

Text copyright © 1993 by Andrea Zimmerman and David J. Clemesha
Illustrations copyright © 1993 by Paul Meisel
Printed in Mexico. All rights reserved.

Library of Congress Cataloging-in-Publication Data
Zimmerman, Andrea Griffing.
   The cow buzzed / by Andrea Zimmerman and David Clemesha ;
illustrated by Paul Meisel.
       p.   cm.
   Summary: The farm animals give one another a cold, passing along
their distinctive voices along with the coughs, sniffles, and sneezes.
   ISBN 0-06-020808-2. — ISBN 0-06-020809-0 (lib. bdg.)
   ISBN 0-06-443410-9 (pbk.)
   [1. Domestic animals—Fiction.   2. Cold (Disease)—Fiction.
3. Animal sounds—Fiction.]   I. Clemesha, David.   II. Meisel, Paul, ill.
III. Title.
PZ7.Z618Co   1993   91-31905
[E]—dc20   CIP
                                                                  AC

Typography by Christine Kettner
❖

To Christian
—AZ and DC

For my parents
—PM

THERE ONCE WAS A FARM where a sensible rabbit and some other animals lived. The rabbit often gave advice like "Don't walk in mud puddles" and "Watch out for bees." But no one ever listened.

One day a little bee flew in to visit the farm. He had a funny little cold. *"Ah-choo!"* he sneezed.

The cow caught the cold. She caught the cough and the sniffle and the sneeze *ah-choo*, and it was odd because she caught the buzz.

"*Buzz buzz,*" said the cow. "*Buzzzzz. Cough cough,
sniffle sniffle, ah-choo!*"

So the pig caught the cold. He caught the cough and the sniffle and the sneeze *ah-choo*, and it's true he caught the moo.

"*Moo, moo,*" said the pig. "*Moooo. Cough cough, sniffle sniffle, ah-choo!*"

moooo

So the duck caught the cold. She caught the cough and the sniffle and the sneeze *ah-choo*, and it wasn't her choice, she caught that voice.

"*Oink, oink,*" said the duck. "*Oiiink. Cough cough, sniffle sniffle, ah-choo!*"

So the dog caught the cold. He caught the cough and the sniffle and the sneeze *ah-choo*. It's a fact, he caught that quack.

"Quack, quack," said the dog. "Quaaack. Cough cough, sniffle sniffle, ah-choo!"

So the rooster caught the cold. He caught the cough and the sniffle and the sneeze *ah-choo*. And hark, he caught the bark.

"Ruff, ruff," said the rooster. *"Rrrruff. Cough cough, sniffle sniffle, ah-choo!"*

So the cat caught the cold. She caught the cough and the sniffle and the sneeze *ah-choo*. And what do you know? She caught his crow.

"*Cock-a-doodle-doo,*" said the cat. "*Cock-a-doodle-doooo. Cough cough, sniffle sniffle, ah-choo!*"

Now the rabbit caught the cold. He caught the cough and the sniffle and the sneeze *ah-choo*, and somehow he caught the meow.

"*Meow, meow,*" said the rabbit. "*Meooow. Cough cough, sniffle sniffle . . .*" but when he went "*ah-choo!*" he covered his mouth. So no one else caught the cold.

When dinnertime came, the cow buzzed, so the farmer gave her honey thinking she was a bee.

"Moo," said the pig, so he got hay.

"Oink," said the duck,
so she got slops.

"Quack," said the dog,
so he got snails.

"*Ruff,*" said the rooster, so he got bones.

"*Cock-a-doodle-doo,*" said the cat, so she got corn.

"*Meow,*" said the rabbit, so he got fish.

Now with all the wrong voices and all the wrong food and all the coughing and sniffling and sneezing, all the animals were getting grumpy.

"It's your fault," meowed the rabbit. "I caught it from you."

"I caught it from you," crowed the cat.

"I caught it from you," barked the rooster.

"I caught it from you," quacked the dog.

"I caught it from you," oinked the duck.

"I caught it from you," mooed the pig.

"I caught it from you," buzzed the cow.

Everyone looked at the little bee. "Who me?"

"Yes, you," said all the animals in their mixed-up voices.

"Where did you catch this cold?"

The little bee took a breath, opened his mouth, and said, *"ROARRRR!"* And he flew back to his home at the zoo.

After a while all the animals on the farm got well.
They stopped coughing and sniffling and sneezing
ah-choo. And they got their own voices back.

The cow said, *"Moo, moo."*

The pig said, *"Oink, oink."*

The duck said, *"Quack, quack."*

The dog said, *"Ruff, ruff."*

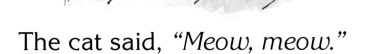

The rooster said, *"Cock-a-doodle-doo."*   The cat said, *"Meow, meow."*

And the rabbit gave advice. He said, "Keep your coughs and sneezes to yourselves." Everyone agreed.

Of course, they still walk in mud puddles whenever they please. But they decided it would be a good idea to watch out for bees.